MW00902319

THIS BOOK IS GIVEN WITH LOVE

To ______________________________

From ______________________________

Written by Leigha Huggins
Illustrated by Stella Mongodi
Edited by Sheri Wall and Sam Cabbage

 Published in the United States
by Puppy Dogs & Ice Cream, Inc.
ISBN: 978-1-956462-09-8
Edition: October 2021

For all inquiries, please contact us at:
info@puppysmiles.org

To see more of our books, visit us at:
www.PuppyDogsAndIceCream.com

A shout out to all the dads deserving of their capes - the human dads, the animal dads, and all the dads I create through illustration.

- STELLA

A dad worthy of a cape is one that shows up with love... I am lucky enough to have both an amazing father and an incredible dad for my own two boys. Thank you to my bonus dad who has taught me more than he will ever know. And a congrats to Anthony on your new cape-wearing journey!

- LEIGHA

WITH YOU,
every memory is new to adore,
from make-believe, gaming,
reading, and more.

As long as you're with me and I'm with you.

SOMETIMES,

I'm in need of a new point of view,
without any delay,
you know just what to do...

FROM LESSONS,

to chatter, to long nature walks,
or trying to out-smell
each other's old socks!

POSSIBILITIES
are endless beyond the bright sky.
Even without wings,
you encourage me to fly.

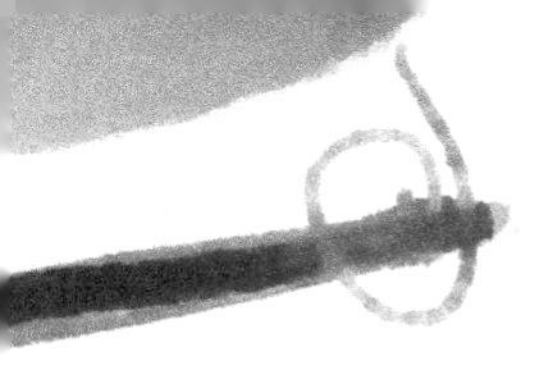

YOU ARE

full of adventure and comical wit.
When you decide to have fun,
you truly commit!

MY FAVORITE
place is right here by your side,
forever your shadow
as we roam in stride.

YOUR STORYTELLING

is the absolute best.
I could listen all night,
but now you need rest.

DAD

I WISH

time together passed slower than slow.
There's never enough time
to learn all that you know.

YOUR PROTECTION
and valor keep me on course,
to be brave and ambitious
with such moral force.

I MAKE

you look good is what you always say.
Yet I'm your true reflection
in every which way.

some emotions you don't always share.
But I know if I need you,
you'll always be there.

I MAY
huff and puff if I don't get my way,
but I'll understand
when I hear what you say.

YOU'RE ALWAYS

a hoot while teaching me more,
giving me wisdom
and the courage to soar!

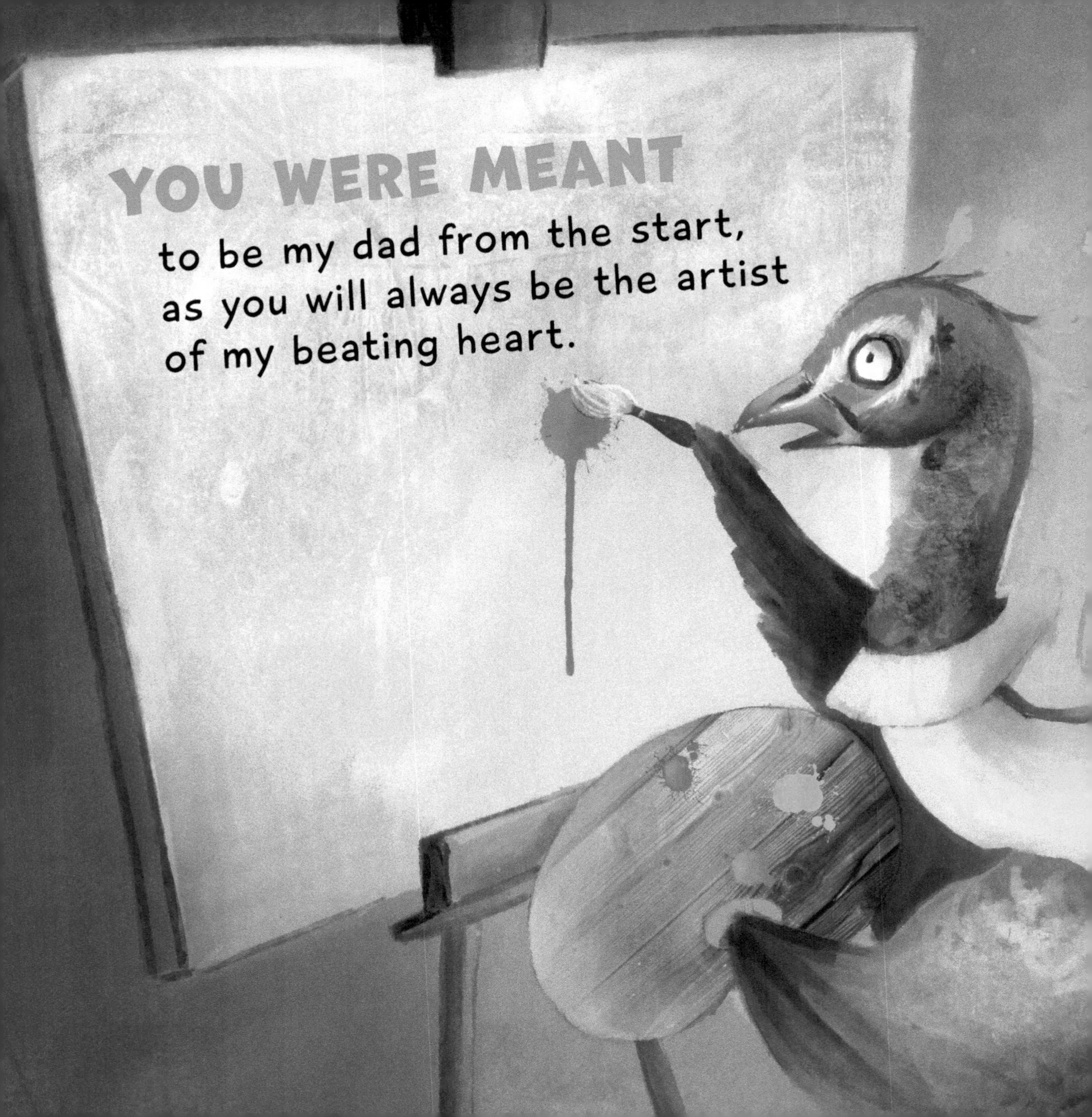
YOU WERE MEANT
to be my dad from the start,
as you will always be the artist
of my beating heart.

I HOPE
that someday,
your cape will fit me.

FOR YOU
are the best hero
there will ever be!

CLAIM YOUR FREE GIFT!

Visit:

PDICBooks.com/Gift

Thank you for purchasing

CAPES ARE FOR DADS

and welcome to the Puppy Dogs & Ice Cream family.
We're certain you're going to love the little gift
we've prepared for you at the website above.

CPSIA information can be obtained
at www.ICGtesting.com
Printed in the USA
BVHW051931270122
627215BV00002B/37